All About Grapes

Denzel T. Carter

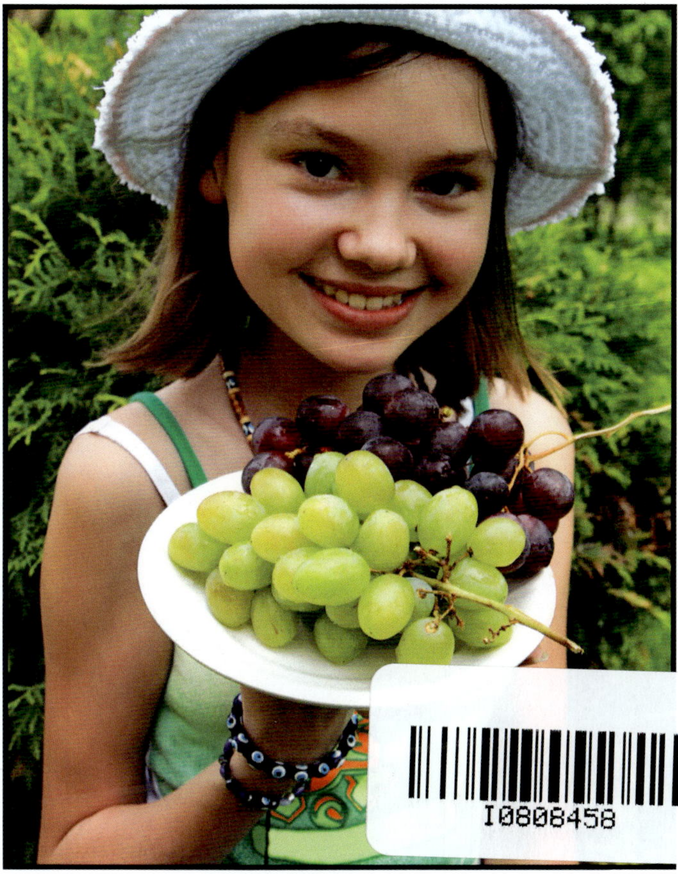

Rosen REAL READERS

Rosen Classroom™
New York

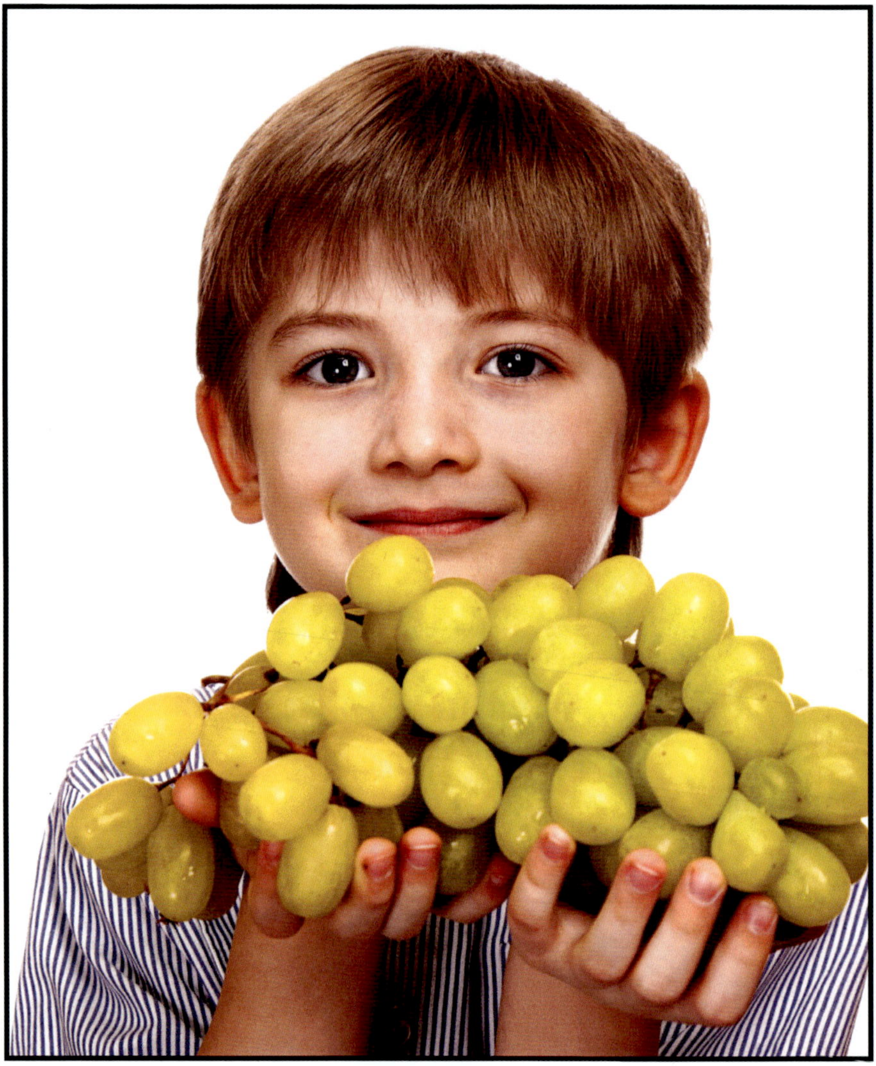

Grapes are a fruit.

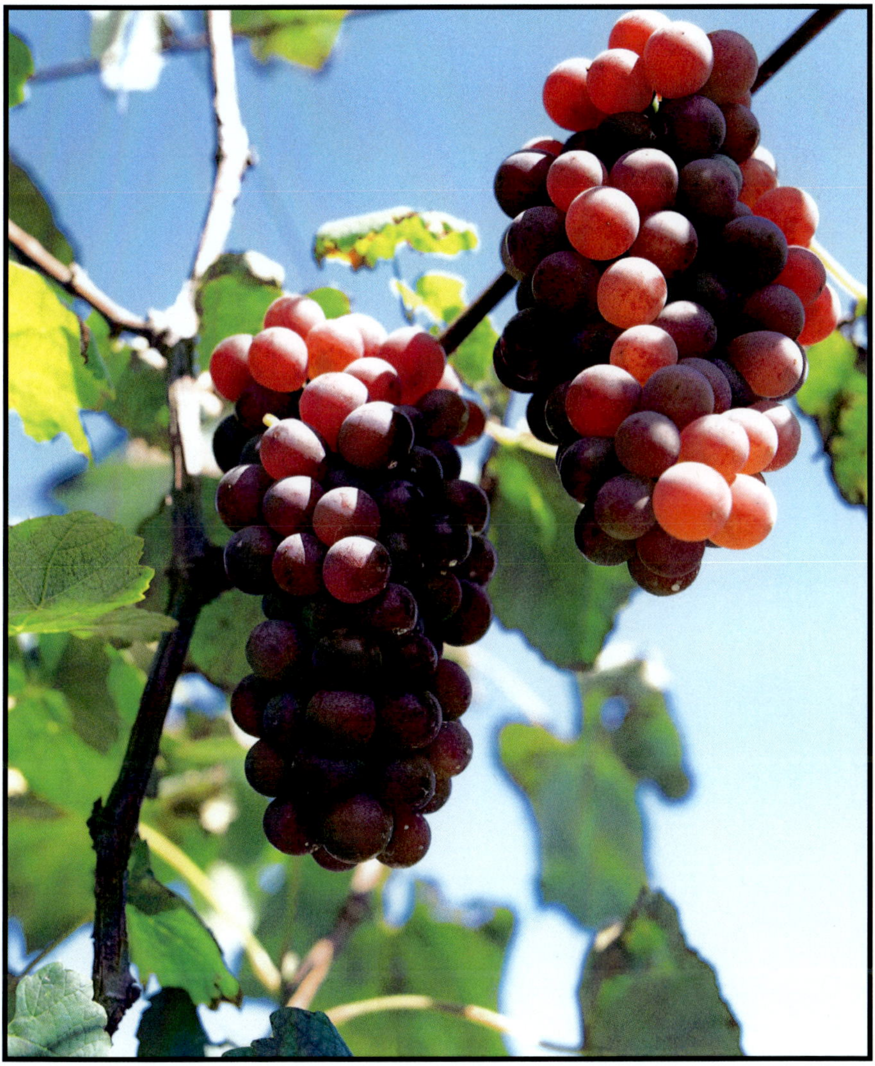

Grapes grow on vines.

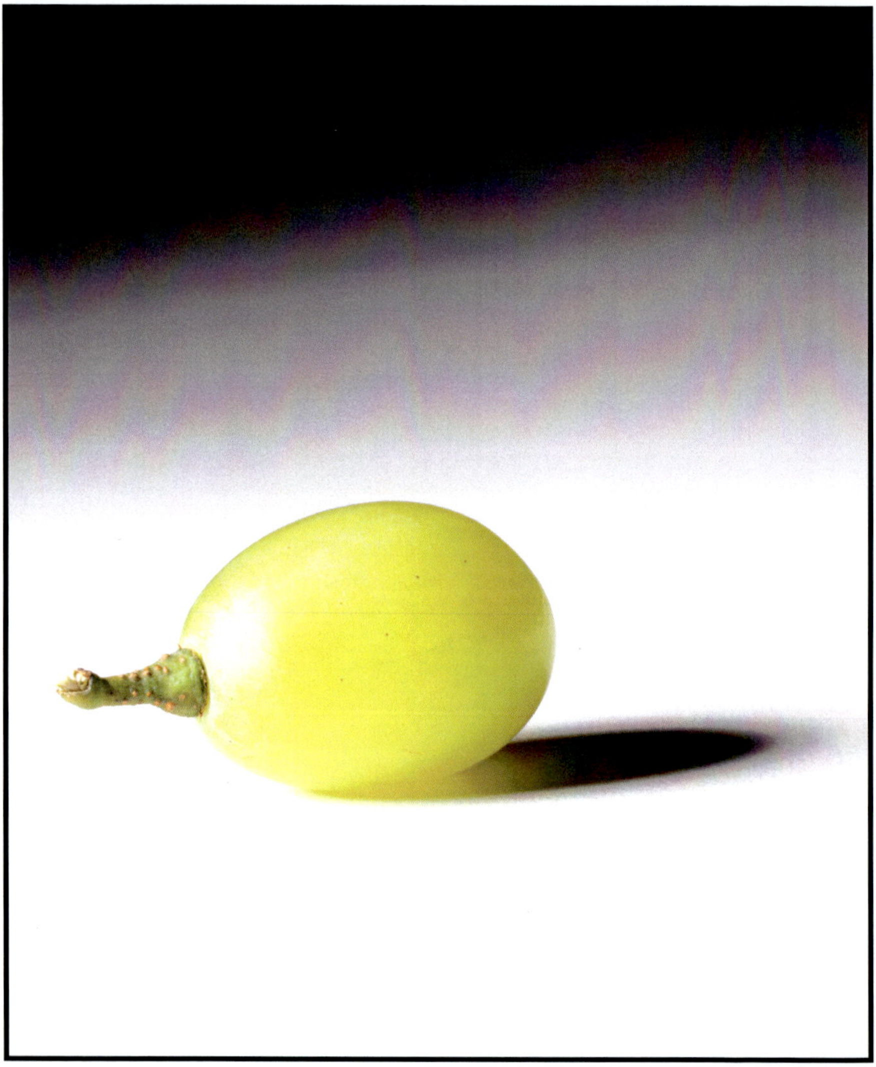

Grapes are small.

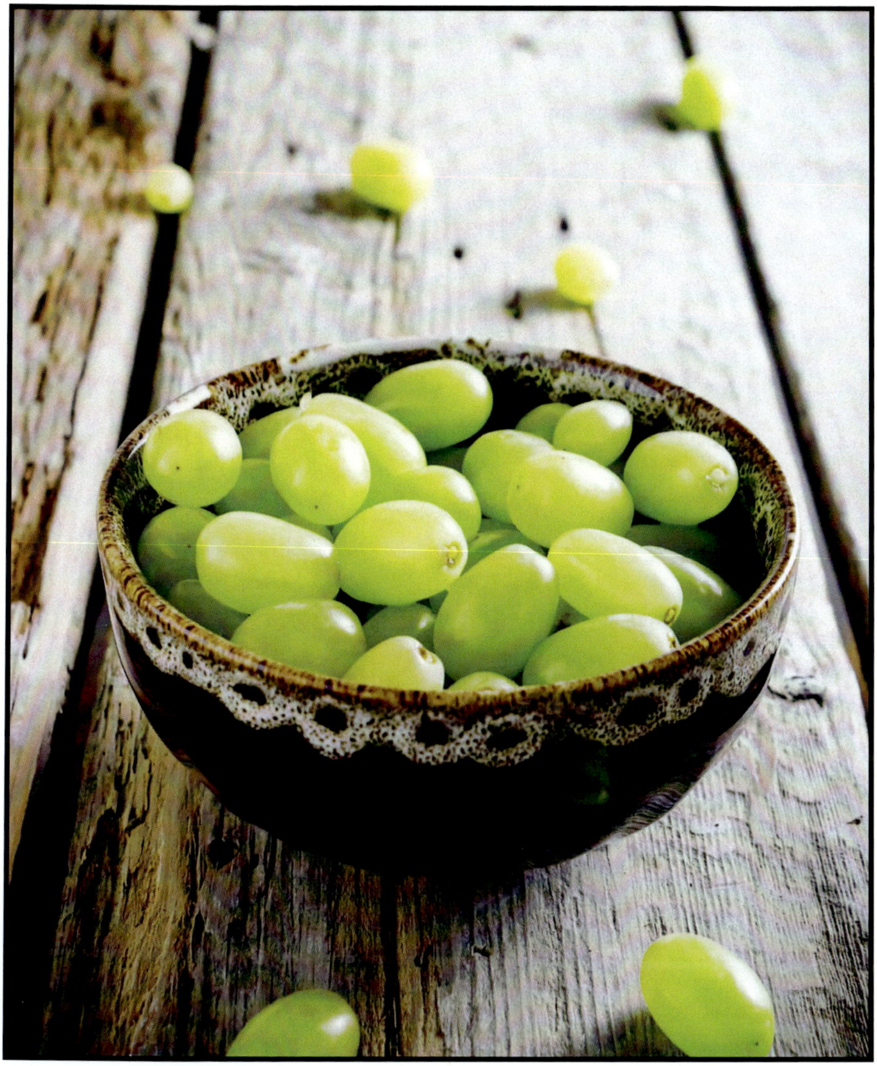

Grapes are green.

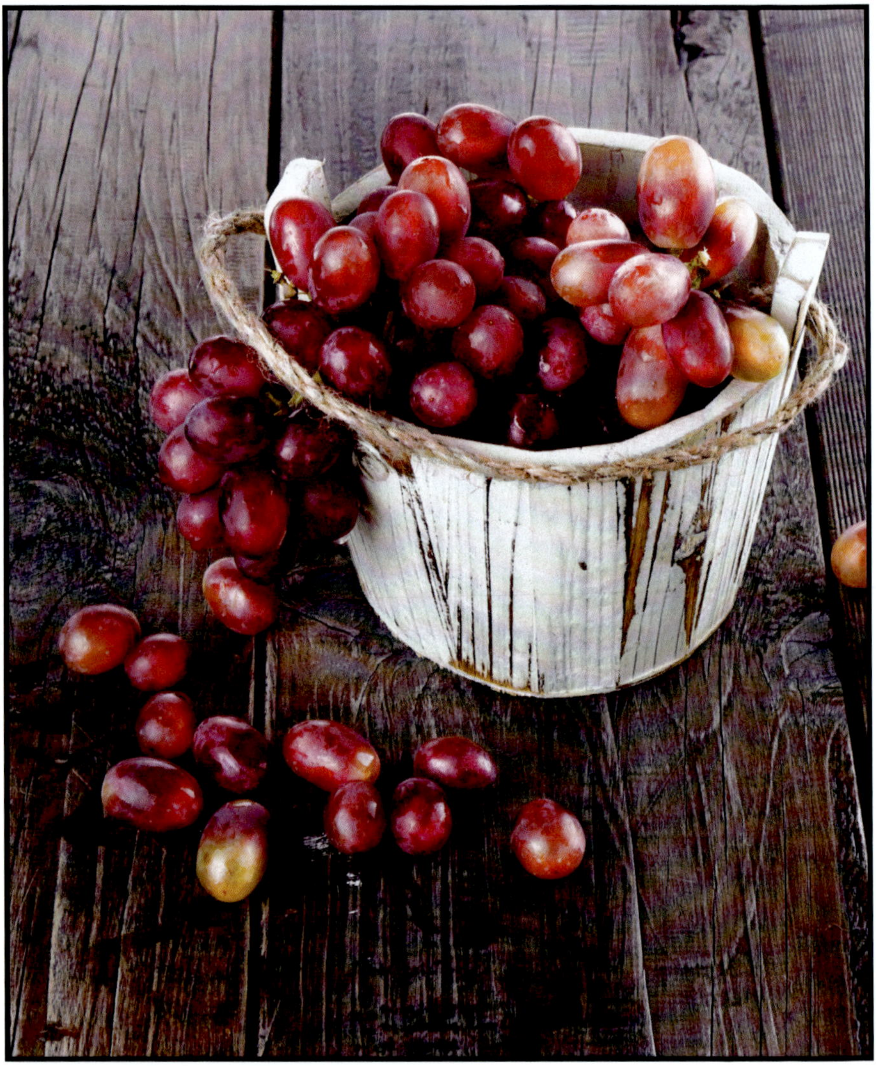

Grapes are purple.

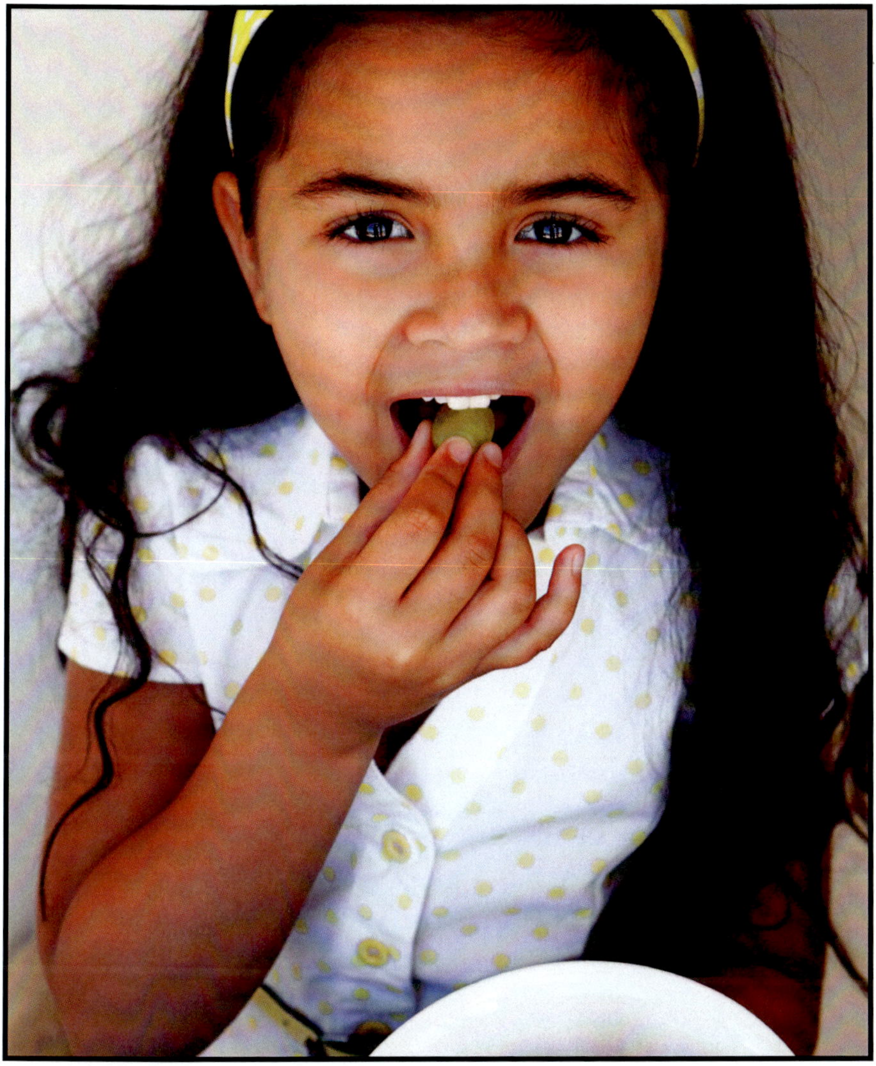

Grapes are good to eat.

Words To Know

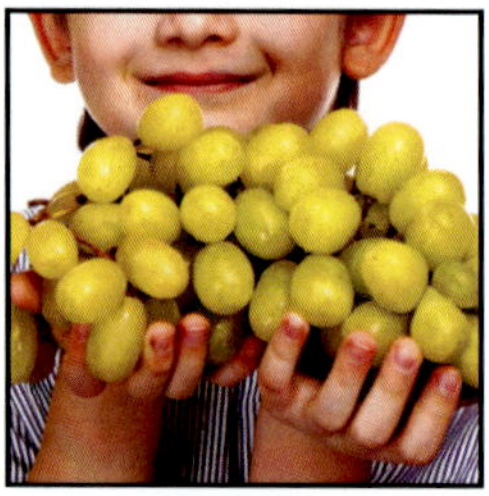

grapes

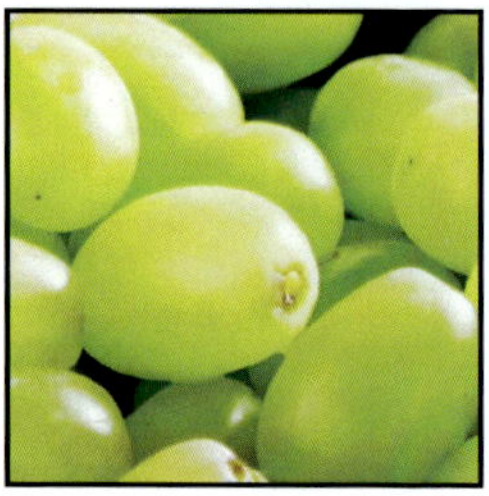

green

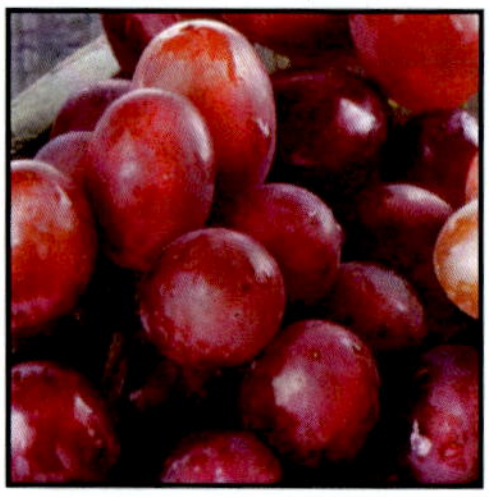

purple

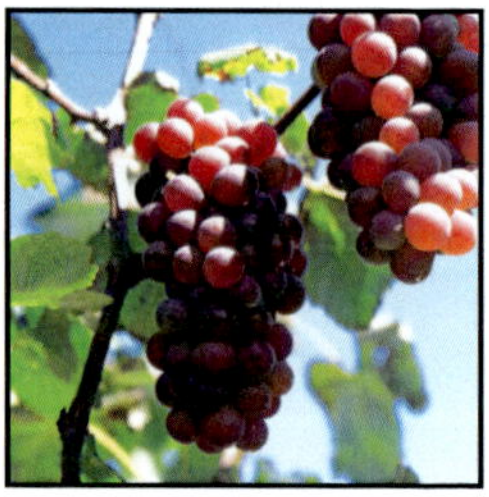

vine